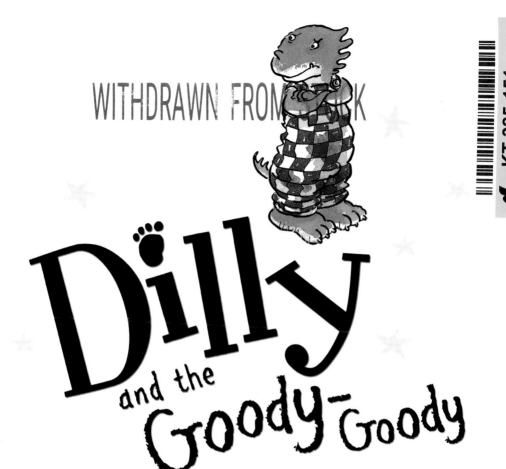

Dilly
and the
Goody-Goody

Reading Ladder

Mother was very cross.

'Oh Dilly,' she said, 'I told you not to make a mess! Our guests will be here any minute.'

'Guests, Mother?' said Dilly.

His toys were spread all over

the sitting room.

'What guests?'

'My friend Diana and her little dinosaur, Dodie,' said Mother.

'They're coming to tea. Remember?'

'No, Mother,' said Dilly.

Don't you ever listen?

7

Mother sighed and rolled her eyes.

Dilly was used to it and took no notice.

But that made Mother even more cross.

She said he had to help tidy up.

8

'Psst, Dilly!' hissed Dorla, Dilly's

big sister. 'Mother's been talking about

Dodie a lot recently...'

'Is Dodie the good little dinosaur?'
said Dilly. 'The one who never does
anything naughty? I thought you
made him up.'

'Well, I didn't,' said Mother, with
a big smile.

10

'He's real, and I'm sure you and Dodie
are going to be great pals. Who knows?
He might even teach you to
behave properly.'

'Fat chance!' muttered Dilly.

'What was that, Dilly?' asked Mother.

'Nothing, Mother,' said Dilly.

Mother gave Dilly a hard look.

But he was saved by the bell.

The front doorbell, that is.

Diana and Dodie had arrived.

'Dorla and Dilly, I'd like you to meet

Diana,' said Mother.

'And this, of course, is Dodie.'

14

'Pleased to meet you, Dorla,' said Diana.

'And you too, Dilly. I've heard so much about you.'

Dilly looked Dodie up and down.

Dodie was very neat and very clean.

He smiled at Dilly.

Dilly didn't smile back.

'Shall we go into the dining room?'
said Mother. 'There are drinks and
swamp-worm cookies and beetle cake...'

What happened next was *awful*.

16

Dilly made lots of disgusting slurping

noises as he drank his juice.

Then he stuffed his cookies and cake in

all at once.

Dodie sat there with his eyes wide

and his mouth open.

'Now that tea is over, Dilly,'

said Mother at last, 'you can take

Dodie out to play in the garden.'

'Do I have to, Mother?' said Dilly.

18

'You most certainly do,' said Mother firmly.

'OK,' sighed Dilly. He got down

from the table and stomped off

into the garden –

STOMP, STOMP, STOMP.

Dodie followed slowly behind.

'What shall we play then?' said Dilly.

He jumped onto his climbing frame

and hung upside down.

'Got any good ideas?'

'Er . . . no,' said Dodie. 'I haven't.'

'You're not much help,' said Dilly.

'I'm sorry,' said Dodie.

Dilly sat up and jumped off the
climbing frame.

'I know,' Dilly said . . .

'How about getting wet?'

'Oh no,' said Dodie, 'I couldn't do that.'

'Well,' said Dilly, 'how about getting dirty?'

'Oh no,' said Dodie, 'I couldn't do that.'

'OK,' said Dilly. 'How about
getting wet and dirty?'
'Oh no,' said Dodie, 'I couldn't
do that.'

'Tell me,' said Dilly, 'What do you
do for fun?'

'I keep my toys tidy,' said Dodie.

'I make sure my books are nice
and neat on the shelf.

I polish my shoes.

I help mother

with the washing up...'

Dilly stood there with

his eyes wide and

his mouth open.

'You know what, Dodie?' Dilly

said at last.

'What, Dilly?' said Dodie.

'You're a real goody-goody.'

'I know,' said Dodie gloomily.

'And I hate it. I'd love to be naughty like you, Dilly, but I just don't know what to do.'

Dilly smiled for the first time that day.

'It's easy-peasy,' said Dilly.

'I'll teach you.'

He taught Dodie how to be naughty with water.

He taught Dodie how to be naughty with dirt.

He taught Dodie how to be naughty with water *and* dirt.

He taught Dodie how to be
naughty in all sort of ways.
And Dodie soon got the
hang of it.

'Watch out,' said Dilly.

'Here comes trouble.'

Mother was marching down

the garden towards them.

'What happens now?' asked Dodie.

'Oh, Mother will probably

tell me off again,' said Dilly.

34

'But that's OK. It means you get to hear my party piece.'

'I can't wait,' said Dodie.

Mother did tell Dilly off. She shouted
and she waved her arms around.

She went dark green in the face.

Dilly let her finish. Then . . .

37

he opened his mouth and fired off an

ultra-special 150-mile-an-hour

super-scream.

'I think we ought to be going home now,'

said Diana when she had recovered.

'Come along, Dodie!'

'But I don't want to,' wailed Dodie.

Then he screamed and swished his

tail around, and threw himself

down and pounded his paws

on the ground.

Diana stood there with

her eyes wide and *her*

mouth open.

Mother gave Dilly a very hard look.

'Psst, Dilly!' hissed Dorla. 'How did
you do it?'

Dilly didn't say anything. He did
give Dodie a thumbs-up sign, though.

And Dodie did the same back to him.

Diana got Dodie to leave at last.

Dilly, alas, behaved badly for the
rest of the day.

43

He emptied his toy cupboard,

he jumped on the sofa,

he broke Mother's best vase,

he argued with Dorla,

he was rude at supper,

BOING!

44

he made the bathroom very wet

and very messy...

and then he ran away and

wouldn't go to bed.

45

But mother caught him in the end.

'I'm glad Dodie came today, Mother,' said

Dilly, when she was tucking him in

at last.

'Can he come again tomorrow?'

Mother stood for a second in the doorway.

Then she smiled. 'Fat chance,' she said.

'Night Dilly.'

'Night, Mother,' said Dilly. Then he

giggled under the covers for ages.